LET'S GO TO A SHOW!

How to Win Ribbons & Have Fun Too

By Lesley Ward

Amy Fox, editor
Nick Clemente, special consultant

Cover and book design by Bocu & Bocu

Library of Congress Cataloging-in-Publication Data
Ward, Lesley.
Let's go to a show : how to win ribbons and have fun too / by Lesley Ward.
   p. cm.
Summary: Informs horse show participants where to sign up for a show,
how to get both horse and rider ready to compete, and what to do upon
arrival.
ISBN 1-889540-85-4 (pbk. : alk. paper)
1. Horse shows--Juvenile literature. 2. Horsemanship--Juvenile
literature. [1. Horse shows. 2. Horsemanship.] I. Title.
SF294.7 .W37 2002
798.2'4--dc21
   2001008433

BowTie™ Press
A Division of Fancy Publications
3 Burroughs
Irvine, California 92618
(949) 855-8822

Printed and Bound in Singapore
10 9 8 7 6 5 4 3 2 1

I would like to thank my wonderful students,
Megan Lynn, Heather Dunham, and Elizabeth Pagan,
because every time I give one of them a lesson,
I learn something new about horses and riding!
—Lesley Ward

CONTENTS

INTRODUCTION

If you love horses and spend a lot of time in the saddle, there's one thing for sure—one day you're going to want to compete in a show. Not only is showing tons of fun but it's also a great way to let everyone see how well you have trained your favorite horse or pony. It also feels wonderful to come home with a lot of ribbons!

Shows are exciting because there's so much going on: riders tacking up their horses; people popping over practice fences; braided ponies cantering by judges; and colorful ribbons hanging on trailers. Just being a spectator can be fun. But if you're like most pony-mad kids, you'll want to be part of the action.

But before you toss your horse in the trailer and head for the show ground, it's important that you and your four-legged friend are 100 percent ready to compete. You'll want your showing experience to be fun—not frustrating—and this book will help you become a showing success.

Read on to find out when you'll be ready to go to a show. Learn about the different show classes and decide which ones are suitable for you and your horse. Feel what it's like to be in a show, and get the lowdown on all of the stuff you have to do before you even enter the ring. You'll also get the inside scoop on what judges are looking for when they watch a class and how you can impress a judge when you're in the ring.

So, what are you waiting for? Give your tack a good cleaning, groom your horse from head to hoof, and polish your boots until they shine. It's show time and you're ready to roll!

You can feel proud of yourself and your favorite horse when you win a ribbon.

CHAPTER ONE

STARTING OUT

The secret to successful showing is being totally prepared. You won't win any ribbons if your horse is badly behaved or if you don't know what you are supposed to do in your class. So, before you head off to compete at your first show, take a few minutes to read what you need to do and ask yourself some questions.

BE A SPECTATOR

Watch a few shows. Take a picnic and a pony pal and make a fun day out of it. Go to the show office and get a schedule so you know what's going on. Watch any classes you think you and your horse might enter in the future. Make a mental note of what the competitors are wearing and what sort of tack the horses are sporting. Are the horses wearing mild snaffle bits? Are they wearing martingales to keep their heads down?

Study the riders in the ring. Try to figure out which rider will win the first place blue ribbon. You can learn a lot from watching other competitors.

Walk around the trailer area and watch people getting their horses ready. Walk over to the warm-up arena and watch people popping over practice fences. Imagine how your horse would act at the show. Listen to the trainers as they help their students. Some of their instructions might relate to you and your horse.

You could also volunteer to help at a show to get the inside scoop about how things work. This would involve opening and closing gates, taking entries, or helping the judge—anything to make yourself useful. You might get a free lunch for helping, and you'll learn a lot too.

If you've got a friend who is already showing, offer to be her groom for the day. Being a groom is tons of fun, and your friend might help you when you go to your first show.

Left: *Being a spectator at a show is a great way to learn about competing.*
Above: *Offer to be a friend's groom for the day. She'll appreciate the help.*

ARE YOU READY TO SHOW?

You should have some riding experience before you go to a show. If you've been riding for only six months, it's not a good idea to enter a jumping class. If you're a new rider, you might consider entering a class or two at a schooling show held for fun at your stable, but don't pack your horse into a trailer and head off to a big show. You're probably not ready yet, but you will be soon!

Before you go to a show, you must be able to walk, trot, and canter a horse safely around other horses. You also must be able to handle a horse if he misbehaves. You can't get scared if he's naughty. You should also know how to groom and tack up your horse without any help.

NO HORSE? NO PROBLEM!

Even if you don't have a horse, you can still compete in shows. If you take lessons, your riding school may let you borrow or "rent" a horse for a show, especially if the show is taking place at the school. You'll be able to groom your horse and braid him if you want. It will be like competing on a horse of your own. Ask your instructor how much it costs to borrow a horse. If a lesson horse is really popular, you'll have to book him a few weeks in advance because everyone else will want to ride him in the show too!

Above: *You must know how to walk, trot, and canter safely before entering a show.*
Right: *You may be able to borrow a horse from your riding school.*

IS YOUR HORSE READY?

Don't even think about going to a show unless your horse will do the following when you're at the barn:

- lead quietly

- tie up to a trailer and not pull back and break his lead rope and halter

- walk, trot, and canter calmly

- work near other horses without kicking or acting grumpy

- stop when you ask him

- stand quietly

WHAT WILL YOU WEAR?

Don't rush out to the tack shop and spend all your money on brand-new show clothes. Check the bulletin board at your barn first because older kids might be selling their outgrown clothes. Also check tack stores for used clothes on consignment. Here is what you should wear:

Helmet: Wear an approved safety helmet with a fixed chinstrap. Most people show in a velvet hunt cap, but if you have a schooling helmet or a jockey skullcap, you can put a black velvet cover on it.

Shirt: Girls wear a ratcatcher. This is a special shirt that comes with a detachable collar. Most girls button the collar to the shirt and many fasten a pretty stock pin on the front. A monogram with your initials on the collar looks great too. Ratcatchers come in different colors and in solids and stripes. Choose one that matches your jacket. Boys wear a shirt and a tie.

Show jacket: Navy blue jackets are always popular, but some competitors wear green, gray, or black. The jacket can be pinstriped or plain. Try to get one that fits you properly.

Jodhpurs or britches: Both are made of stretchy material. Most people wear beige jodhpurs or britches at shows. Jodhpurs are long and go down to your ankles. They are worn with short boots. If you wear jodhpurs, wear garters (leather straps that go around your leg under your knee). They keep your jodhpurs in place. Britches go down to just below the knee and are worn with tall boots.

Left: *Jodhpurs and garters are suitable for younger riders.*
Above: *Your showing helmet must have a fixed chinstrap.*

Tall boots or short boots: If you are younger than thirteen and you are small, you can wear jodhpurs, garters, and short boots. Most young people wear short boots that lace up the front (paddock boots), zip up or pull on. If you're a bit older, you should wear tall boots and britches. You can wear plain boots or field boots (boots with laces that tie up in the front). Your showing boots should be black. If you're just starting out, you can wear rubber boots, but as you become more experienced and start going to bigger shows, you'll need to buy leather boots.

Gloves: Wear black gloves. They can be leather, which are the most expensive, or cloth, the least expensive. Gloves give you extra grip, plus they camouflage your hands if you have to tug on the rein to get your horse to turn!

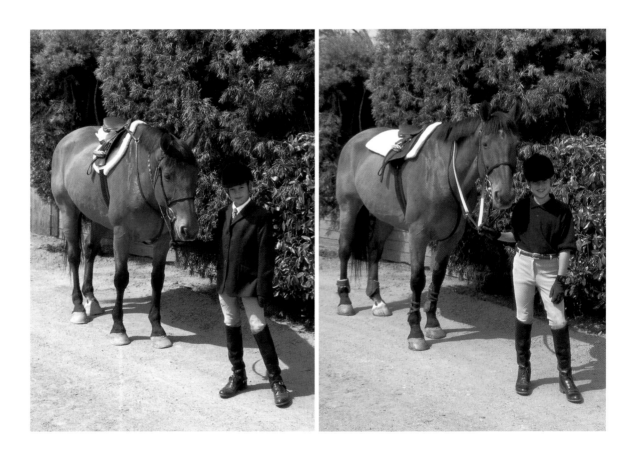

Above Left: *Teenage competitors should wear tall boots.*
Above Right: *A solid polo shirt is suitable attire for a jumper class.*
Opposite: *A hair net keeps your hair neatly under your helmet.*

HAIR TIPS

Your hair should be neat and tidy under your helmet. Boys, trim your hair. Girls, if you are younger than twelve years old and have long hair, put it in two tight braids. If you're older, keep your hair under your cap. Here's the best way to do it:

1. Put your hair in a low ponytail using an elastic band.

2. Flip the end of the ponytail up so it rests on top of your head. Secure it with a bobby pin or a clip.

3. Hold your hair in place with a hair net.
   If the net is too big, make a knot in it.

4. Gently slip your hat on from back to front. Squeeze any wispy hairs back under the helmet. Very stylish!

YOUR HORSE'S TACK

Keep your tack simple at a horse show. Judges don't like colorful saddle pads or neon-pink boots or bandages. Most horses compete in brown-leather tack. Equitation or hunter class judges like the "traditional look." They don't like black or synthetic tack.

Here's what an equitation or hunter horse should wear:

- A brown-leather saddle; most people use fairly flat jumping saddles

- A brown-leather girth
- A fluffy white saddle pad that is shaped like the saddle
- A brown-leather bridle with a plain noseband. Flashes or dropped nosebands are not allowed in hunter classes. Show bridles should be plain, without brass or white fittings. The reins should be plain or braided. Don't use rubber reins in hunter classes.
- A mild snaffle bit such as an egg-butt, a D-ring, or a full-cheek. If you ride a very strong pony, you could use a stronger Kimberwicke bit in cross-rail, beginner rider, or short-stirrup classes. Pelham bits can use a bit converter, which is a leather strap that attaches to the bit and allows you to ride with one rein instead of two.
- A standing martingale: The kind that fastens to your horse's noseband. Check the shows in your area. Some people may not use a martingale at all. A running martingale—the kind that fastens to the reins—is not allowed in hunter classes. If your horse is wearing one, you'll be disqualified.

Left: *Use brown-leather tack in hunter classes.* Top: *A mild, D-ring snaffle is suitable for a hunter class.* Bottom: *An egg-butt snaffle is used a lot in hunter classes.* Opposite: *You can use a flash noseband in a jumper class but not a hunter class.*

Judges are less picky in jumper classes. You may spot strong bits, such as gags or Pelhams, and running martingales in jumper classes. You will also see different types of saddles and breastplates to help keep the saddles in place while the horse is zipping around the course at top speed.

You may see a horse wearing boots in a jumper class. Support boots are not worn in hunter and equitation classes.

If you're going to a very small fun show, don't panic and go out and buy new tack. Your tack should be fine as long as it's clean and in good condition. Synthetic tack is fine for small beginners' shows.

EXTRA EQUIPMENT

CROP: If your horse is lazy, carry a small brown or black crop. Don't carry a long crop or one that is a bright color.

SPURS: Only wear spurs if you know how to use them and your trainer agrees that you should wear them.

CHAPTER TWO

FINDING A SHOW

Once you and your parents have decided that you and your horse are ready to go to a show, find out what shows are taking place near your barn. If you have a trainer, he or she should know about any shows coming up.

If you keep your horse at a boarding barn, check the barn bulletin board. There should be notices advertising upcoming events. If you board at a fairly big stable, there may be regular shows on the premises.

Look for local freebie horse magazines in tack shops and feed stores. Most of them have calendars of local events. Show organizers also post notices about their events in tack shops and feed stores, or they leave a lot of prize lists or programs for customers to take home. Grab the ones that look interesting, and when you get home look them over carefully to see if there are any classes you want to enter. Show them to your trainer too. Your trainer might think you are ready for a class that you haven't even considered!

THE SHOW GROUND

If you've never been to the place where the show is going to be held, do some investigating. Ask your trainer or your horsey friends if they've ever been to the show ground. You don't want to arrive at the show and discover that the barn is falling down, there's not enough parking, and the show jumps are rickety and unsafe!

The barn hosting the show should have a good reputation. The show ground should be neat and tidy. There should be a large showing ring with good footing and a fence around it, and a safe, enclosed area where riders can warm up. Plus, there must be plenty of space where you can park a trailer and tie up your horse. If you have to park in a grassy field, look around for trees to park under. It's nice to park in the shade at summer shows! Don't go to a show if the only available parking is on concrete. It's not comfortable for your horse to stand on a hard surface for hours and hours.

Left: *Tack shops often post notices about local shows.*
Top: *The show ground should have a fenced arena.*
Bottom: *A show should have a large warm-up area.*

RATED SHOWS

Some shows are rated by USA Equestrian (formerly the American Horse Show Association), a big organization that regulates different types of equestrian activities all over the United States. It helps to organize more than 2,500 shows annually. The USA Equestrian-rated shows tend to be well run and are held at nice show grounds. The USA Equestrian shows also have strict rules, so you always know what to expect, but entry fees can be expensive.

The USA Equestrian shows have different ratings: A, B, and C. A-shows are the biggest and have the toughest competition. They are for riders, both kids and adults, who have a lot of showing experience and talented horses and ponies.

If you win a ribbon in a class at a rated show, you may earn points toward a year-end award. This means that if you win the same class at a different show, you earn more points and you might get a trophy at the end of the year. Very cool!

Above: *The competition can be tough at a rated show.*
Right: *Measure your pony before you enter a rated show.*

Some rated shows are very big and held over several days or weeks. The competition can be tough because most of the riders are experienced, and the horses and ponies competing are often high-class animals who are worth a lot of money.

HEIGHT CARDS

If you're going to compete a pony in USA Equestrian-recognized shows, then you must have him measured by two officials from USA Equestrian at his first rated show. The officials will give you a temporary card stating your pony's height. You will receive a permanent card in the mail. You must take this card with you to every USA Equestrian show because officials can question your pony's height at any time. They don't want a 12.3 hands high (hh) pony competing in a class for ponies 12.2 hh and under.

DRUGS

If your horse is on some sort of medication or supplement, for example to treat his arthritis, you must make sure that the medicine and the amount that you give him is approved by USA Equestrian. Show veterinarians give random blood tests to horses at big shows, and if your horse is found to have too

much of a certain drug in his bloodstream, you could be disqualified and fined. If you're a member of USA Equestrian, you'll be sent a booklet that tells you which drugs and supplements are allowed at shows and which aren't. Make sure your trainer and parents read the booklet.

UNRATED SHOWS

Unrated shows are often called "open" or "schooling" shows, and they may offer English and western classes. They can be just as organized as rated shows, but they're usually not as big. Unrated shows are perfect for young riders just starting out in the showing world and for green, inexperienced horses.

Schooling shows are not as formal as rated shows. You don't have to have all the fancy showing gear, your horse doesn't have to be perfectly behaved, and the judge may give you helpful pointers about your performance. Entry fees are less expensive than at rated shows.

OTHER TYPES OF SHOWS

Many breed organizations hold their own special shows so that proud owners can show off their horses and ponies. Breed shows are only for registered horses of a certain breed. For example, the American Quarter Horse Congress, held every October, is for horses registered with the American Quarter Horse Association. Breed shows have all sorts of classes, including in-hand and ridden.

Youth shows are for riders who are eighteen years and under.

FILLING OUT FORMS

Once you've decided what classes you'd like to try, you can usually pay your entry fee early. Fill out the entry form and mail a check to the show organizer. Other shows let you pay on the day. Sometimes, if you wait until the day of the show, the entry fee is more, but only by a dollar or two. If you're positive that you're going to a show, pay in advance. Then you won't have to waste time standing in line at the office on a busy show day.

Left: *A schooling show is a great place to start your horse's showing career.*
Above: *Show off your flashy paint horse at a breed show.*

GETTING TO THE SHOW

Once you've chosen a show, you must figure out how you're going to get your horse there. If you have a trailer, you're lucky. If you have a friend with a trailer, you could be lucky. Your friend might take you if you offer to split the expenses of gas and food. If you go with a friend, be a helpful trailer mate so your buddy will want to take you again. Offer to muck out the trailer after the show, or take along drinks and sandwiches to share.

Your trainer might be willing to take you for a fee or might know of someone at your barn who hauls horses. This person may charge you a flat fee or by the mile. Barn bulletin boards often have hauling ads on them.

Some trainers hire a professional hauling company with a huge trailer to take their students' horses to a show. You're expected to share in the hiring costs, which can be quite expensive.

TRAINER TIME

If you have a regular trainer, you might want him or her to come to the show to help you. Most trainers charge for spending the day with you at a show. You may be able to split the fee with other students. Let your trainer know when and where the show is well in advance, and tell him or her what classes you want to enter.

Above: *Ask a friend with a trailer if you can hitch a ride to a show.*
Right: *Your trainer may come to a show to help you.*

CHAPTER THREE

CLASSES

Before you go to a show, decide what classes you want to enter. If you haven't jumped at all, don't enter a jumping class. If your horse is a slowpoke, then a top-speed jumping class is not for you. Read the program. It should have descriptions of each class. If you still have questions, call the show organizer or talk to your trainer.

Here are some classes that you might recognize on a show program:

LEAD-LINE CLASS

The lead-line class is for young riders, usually under the age of eight. An older child or an adult leads the rider's pony. The rider must sit on the horse correctly, should hold on to the reins properly, and must know how to steer and stop. The rider should be in showing gear and helmet, and the leader should look neat and professional.

WALK-TROT CLASS

In a walk-trot class, you walk around the ring until the judge asks you to trot. You are expected to know how to post on the correct diagonal, and you might not win a ribbon if the judge spots you on the wrong diagonal. After a while, the ring steward brings you back to the walk and asks you to change direction. Then you walk and trot on the other rein. Remember to change your diagonal when you change direction!

Left: *Make sure that you are on the correct diagonal in a walk-trot class.*
Right: *A lead-line class is perfect for little sisters and brothers.*

CROSS-RAIL AND TROTTING-POLE CLASSES

Cross-rail and trotting-pole jumping classes are for beginner riders or people riding very green horses. Usually there are either four poles on the ground or four fences, two on each long side of the arena. The fences are cross-rails, usually no more than 1 1/2 foot high. At most shows you'll trot or canter twice around the jumps. Stick to the same gait all the way around the course. There may also be a flat class for cross-rail competitors only.

BEGINNER HORSE OR BEGINNER RIDER CLASSES

These classes are for people who can jump higher than cross-rails but are still learning the ropes. The course is simple, usually

DIVISION CLASSES

Division classes, or divisions, are several classes that are linked together. Points are awarded for every ribbon won in a division. Most divisions have one flat class and two jumping classes. If you win ribbons in each class you could earn enough points to win a ribbon and maybe even a small trophy as the division champion or reserve champion.

made up of simple vertical fences (fences made up of two poles directly on top of each other) that are no higher than about two feet. If you or your horse has won a blue ribbon in other classes, you may not be allowed to compete in beginner horse or rider classes. There will probably be a flat class for beginner horse and rider competitors. In this class, you'll be asked to walk, trot, and canter.

SHORT-STIRRUP CLASSES

The short-stirrup division is open to kids younger than twelve years old. There is usually a flat class and two jumping classes in this division. On the flat, everybody is asked to walk, trot, and canter in both directions. The judge looks at the way you ride—your style and effectiveness in the saddle. The judge will check to see that you are on the correct diagonal when you trot and the correct lead when you canter.

The fences in short-stirrup jumping classes are about 2 feet (or 2 feet 3 inches) high, and you must canter around the course. The fences can be verticals, small walls, and spreads (also called oxers), which are wider fences made up of two poles in which the first pole is lower and slightly more forward than the second pole. The course may also have a roll top—a solid wall with a rounded top.

Left Top: *Cross-rail classes usually have very small fences.*
Left Bottom: *Beginner horse or rider classes may have small but solid fences.*
Right: *Short-stirrup classes are for kids twelve and under.*

EQUITATION CLASSES

In an equitation class, the judge looks at the rider, not the horse. A rider with a good position—quiet hands, secure seat, and strong legs—will place over one who is yanking on his or her horse's mouth. There are classes under saddle (riding on the flat or without obstacles) and classes over fences in the equitation division.

In the under-saddle classes, you'll be asked to walk, trot, and canter. In the classes over fences, it is important that your horse takes off at the correct point in front of a fence and that you're with him all the way. If your horse jumps big and you get

"left behind" the motion and move out of jumping position, you'll be marked down. You'll lose points if your horse taps a fence, knocks down a pole, or refuses to jump.

HUNTER CLASSES

The horse is the one being judged in hunter classes. The judge watches to see if your horse is obedient and well mannered. The judge notes the way your horse moves. Does he zoom around one second and plod around the next, or is his pace steady and even? Hunter classes are for horses who are happy in their work and show it by keeping their ears pricked and their mind on their job.

In the under-saddle hunter classes, you'll be expected to walk, trot, and canter in both directions. The USA Equestrian rule book states that light contact on your

Above: *Your riding skills are judged in an equitation class.*
Right: *Your pony's way of going is judged in a hunter class.*

horse's or pony's mouth is required. Hunter courses are fairly simple and usually have eight or nine jumps. The fences aren't very fancy and will be natural colors like white and brown. You may have to jump "brush fences," which are fences decorated with evergreen branches. You may also have to jump a small wooden gate.

The Pony Hunters division is split into three sections:
- small—12.2 hh and under
- medium—13.2 hh and under
- large—14.2 hh and under

FAULTS

Faults are penalties that the judge gives you for mistakes you have made in the ring while competing. Faults are what knock you out of the ribbons! In equitation classes, you may receive faults for poor rider position, wrong diagonals, wrong leads, bad steering, refusals, and knockdowns.

In hunter classes, you may receive faults if your horse moves badly, has poor jumping style, wiggly approaches to fences, an uneven pace, wrong leads, knockdowns, and refusals.

In jumper classes, you are given faults if you have a runout or a knockdown, or if you don't finish the jumping course within the time limit assigned to the class. You get three faults for the first refusal and six faults for the second refusal. You are eliminated after the third refusal. If your horse knocks down a pole, you get four faults. And finally, if you go off course during a jumping round, you are eliminated and must leave the ring.

While the judge is watching you, he or she makes notes on a card about your performance in the ring. At the end of the class, he or she looks at the card to remember your ride or jumping round and then places you in the class.

JUMPER CLASSES

Jumper courses usually have nine or ten fences. The fences are usually colorful and can sometimes look spooky to a horse. You might see a red wall or a green roll-top obstacle in the arena.

In a jumper class, getting clear around the course in the time allowed is the only thing on which you are judged. The judge does not look at your style or your horse's behavior. If you and your horse get around the course without knocking down a pole or having a refusal, you'll compete in a timed jump-off against other people who have also cleared the course.

A jump-off has fewer fences than the jumper class. The most important thing in a jump-off is speed! People cut corners and jump fences at any angle to save time. The fastest clear round wins.

Jumper classes are less formal than hunter or equitation classes. Competitors often wear polo shirts and no jacket.

SCHOOLING AND WARM-UP CLASSES

Schooling and warm-up classes are usually held at the beginning of the show. They are a chance for you and your horse to pop over a course before your classes begin. The heights will vary in a warm-up class, but there should be one that's right for you and your horse.

Left: *Getting around fast and clear is your goal in a jumper class.*
Above: *Show off your horse's trot in a go-as-you-please class.*

GO AS YOU PLEASE, OR COUNTRY PLEASURE

This is a fun class because you compete at your favorite gait. You walk around the ring until the steward says, "Go as you please," or "Take your favorite gait." Then you can walk, trot, or canter until he or she tells you to stop. If your horse has a lovely smooth canter, you should show it off. You might win the class!

PLEASURE CLASSES

In pleasure classes, your horse is judged on manners and performance. The judge will look at your horse and think, *Hmm, is he a pleasure to ride?* You need to ride with a fairly loose rein in a pleasure class, and you'll be expected to walk, trot, and canter in both directions. Don't forget to smile!

MEDAL CLASSES

These are extra-special classes in which you're judged on your horsemanship, both on the flat and over fences. They usually take place at big shows, although county and regional clubs offer medal classes too.

Qualifying classes are offered at shows throughout the year. There are a different number of first-place finishes needed, depending on your region's qualifying guidelines.

If you win enough first-place ribbons, you qualify for a regional final. If you place at the regional competition, you win a spot at the prestigious National Horse Show finals in Harrisburg, Pennsylvania.

You can also compete in a Maclay Class national final, which is a year-long horsemanship competition. Placing in the top positions at the regional final assures you a spot in this national, which has been held at New York City's famous Madison Square Garden in the past.

SHOWMANSHIP

This is usually an in-hand class, which means that you don't ride your horse in the arena—you lead your horse by holding the reins. The judge looks at you and your horse from head to hoof in a showmanship class, checking to see how clean your horse, tack, and clothing are. Your horse's tack and your clothes must fit well, and your pony must shine like a new penny. If you know how to braid your horse's mane and tail, do it. The person who looks the most professional should win the blue ribbon.

Your pony must sparkle from head to hoof in a showmanship class.

CHAPTER FOUR

GETTING READY

Keep the day before a show free. You have a lot to do, and you don't want to rush. You can ride your horse, but don't tire him out. Just school him and pop over a few fences. If you're jumping the next day, jump a small course or practice a couple of lines (two fences close together). An hour or so in the saddle is okay, but don't go on a four-hour trail ride and wear him out so he has no energy on show day!

SNIP, SNIP

Before going to a show, give your horse a quick trim. Start by tidying up his bridle path, the place where the headpiece sits behind the ears. Trim a section about 1 1/2 inch long close to his head like a crew cut.

Next, trim the whiskers around his muzzle. Use scissors or small trimming clippers. Trim back the hair under his throat too— you don't want him to look like a billy goat.

Never trim the wispy whiskers near his eyes. They protect him. If your horse has a lot of hairs sticking out of his ears, trim them too, but watch that you don't trim the hair inside the ear because it protects the inner ear from flies and dirt. Hold the two sides of the ear together and trim only the hair that's

sticking out. Finally, trim the feathers, the fluffy hair on the back of the legs near the pasterns. Hold the scissors vertically and cut up or down the leg. Don't cut across the leg because the hair will look chopped and messy. Snip away the short hair around the coronet band at the top of the hoof.

If your horse is usually clipped all over (a body clip) and is starting to look fuzzy, you might want to ask an experienced person to reclip him a couple of days before the show so he looks neat and tidy.

Left: *Trim the whiskers around your horse's muzzle.*
Above: *Snip off the feathers on your horse's legs.*

BATH TIME

Give your horse a bath the day before the show—not on show day. Bathing strips natural oils from your horse's skin. These oils make his coat shine. Bathing him the day before allows his coat time to get some shine back. If your horse is gray or pinto, you may have to bathe him on show day because it's almost impossible to keep horses with these color of coats clean!

Use a mild human shampoo or buy horse shampoo from the tack store. There are shampoos formulated for individual coat colors, such as bay or chestnut. If your horse is gray, try one of the special purple whitening shampoos. These shampoos really make a gray horse glow. Use a big, soft sponge and work up a lather on grass and manure stains.

If your horse has a gray mane and tail that turns yellow, use a purple whitening shampoo. Lather up the hair and leave the shampoo on for a few minutes. Rinse the shampoo off and the yellow stain should be gone. Follow the shampoo with a conditioner to make the hair extra soft and manageable.

If you're going to braid your horse on the same day that you bathe him, don't wash his mane. A squeaky clean mane is difficult to braid.

Let your horse dry completely before putting him out in his field or in his stable. Wet horses love to roll and get dirty again!

Left: *Give your pony a bath the day before a show.*
Right: *Here are the tools you need for quick and easy braids.*

If you want to keep your horse superclean after a bath, put a lightweight summer sheet or blanket on him so if he lies down in the stable he won't get dirty. If you keep him outside, put a light turnout rug on him and hope that he stays clean!

If on show day you discover a spot or two on your horse, spray the stain with some stain remover, then wipe it away with a clean cloth. There are several stain removers on the market that you can buy at a tack shop or feed store.

BRAIDING A MANE

Braiding a horse's mane makes him look special, and shows off his neck and head, but it's not required at every show. People rarely braid for schooling shows, but if you want to you can. If you plan to braid for a show, start thinning out, or pulling, the mane a few weeks before. Your horse's mane won't look nice if it's long and shaggy. Pull his mane after you've ridden him when he's still warm. The hair will come out easier if your horse's pores are open. The mane should be pulled to a length of 4 to 6 inches.

Practice braiding in the weeks before a show. Becoming good takes a lot of practice, and once you become good, all your friends will want you to braid their horses!

If you have time, you can braid your horse the morning of a show, but if it takes you a while, braid the night before. With luck, most of the braids will stay in place—especially if you spray some hair spray on them. You may have to redo one or two the next morning. You can also separate the mane into different sections, braid them, and leave them as they are. The next morning roll them into balls, or button braids, and fasten them into place.

Some people braid using yarn (especially at USA Equestrian shows or other big events), but if you're going to a little show, the easiest way to braid is with tiny rubber braiding bands that you buy at the tack shop. Make sure the rubber band is the same color as your horse's mane.

BRAIDING TOOLS

Here are some items that come in handy when you braid:

- **braiding bands**
- **bucket of clean water**
- **hair spray**
- **human hair gel**
- **mounting block, or something to stand on**
- **small mane-pulling comb**
- **sponge**
- **spray bottle full of water**

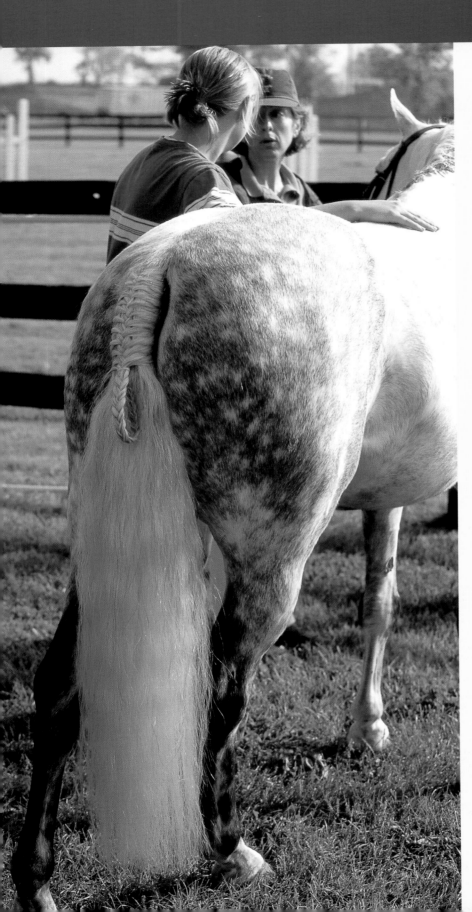

SIMPLE BUTTON BRAIDS

Braiding your horse's mane into small, round buttons is the easiest braiding method. (See photos on p. 43)

1. Brush the mane over to the horse's right side (the opposite side you mount on) and get rid of any tangles.

2. Dip a sponge into water and wet the mane with it. Braiding is easier if the mane is wet. Keep a water bottle handy to moisten dry sections.

3. Squirt some hair gel into your hand and work it into the wet mane.

4. Separate the mane into sections, each about 1-inch wide. Band each section to keep it in place.

5. Starting at the section closest to your horse's ears, separate the first section into three parts, then braid it down to the bottom. Secure the braid tightly with a braiding band.

6. Fold the braid under once, then loop it under again until it forms a small, neat button near the top of the neck. Secure the button with another braiding band. Pop another band on top for extra security.

7. Move on to the second section. If it has dried out too much, spray it with the water bottle.

8. Work your way down the neck. Try to keep all the buttons the same size.

9. Spray the buttons with hair spray to help keep them in place.

Braiding a tail is a skill that takes lots of practice.

Brush then dampen your pony's mane with water.

Gel and separate the mane into small, even sections.

Make sure the braids are tight.

Loop the braid up twice to form a small, neat button.

Secure the button with a braiding band.

All done! That was easy!

43

BRAIDING A TAIL

Tails are braided only for bigger shows, and that's a good thing because braiding a tail can be tricky! The tail hair is woven into a French braid that runs down to the middle of the tail. Then it's looped back and sewn in place. If you want to learn how to braid a tail, ask an experienced braider to show you how to do it. You can often pay someone to braid your horse's mane and tail for you.

CLEAN YOUR TACK AND CLOTHING

Clean your tack the day before the show. Take it apart and wipe it with a damp sponge. Then rub saddle soap into the leather with the sponge. Buff the tack with a dry cloth to make the leather really shine. Drop the bit and stirrups in a bucket of water and clean them with a sponge. If your stirrups have white rubber pads in them, soak them in water with a few drops of bleach to whiten them. Toss your saddle pad in the washing machine to clean it.

Remember to brush off your helmet and to polish your boots before you go to a show. Using a piece of sticky tape, remove any lint or hair on your jacket. Make sure your jodhpurs and shirt are clean too.

Above: *Always clean your tack before a show.* Top Right: *Give your boots a polish so they shine.* Bottom Right: *Make a list so you won't forget important items, such as your horse's Coggin's test.*

MAKE A LIST

It's a terrific idea to make a list of things you need to take to the show. Check the list on the morning of the show to make sure you have everything packed in the car or trailer. Here are some things that should be on your list:

- boots
- braiding kit (in case one of the braids comes undone)
- bridle
- bucket
- camera and plenty of film (If you win a ribbon, Mom or Dad will want to take a picture or two. If your family has a video camera, bring that along too. It's always fun to watch your classes after the show to see what you did right—or wrong!)
- clean, soft cloth for a last-minute boot polish
- crop
- girth
- gloves
- grooming kit
- hay and hay net
- helmet
- money for the entry fee
- riding clothes
- saddle and pad
- treats, such as carrots and apples
- two halters and lead ropes (an extra halter comes in handy if your horse breaks his at the show)
- vaccination records
- water (you can buy a plastic five-gallon

gas tank at a discount store and use it to haul water)
- your horse or pony!

The show secretary may ask to see copies of your horse's vaccination records and his Coggin's test (some shows require that you bring along a Coggin's test). This is a piece of paper that your veterinarian gives you after he does a blood test on your horse to make sure that he doesn't have equine infectious anemia, a highly contagious virus. Make a few copies of the negative test and bring a copy to the show.

CHAPTER FIVE

IT'S SHOW TIME!

Set out early on the day of the show. Give yourself plenty of time in case there's a problem or two along the way. Your horse might not get in the trailer, or your truck might get a flat tire. Try to arrive about an hour and a half before your class so you have plenty of time to pay your entry fees and warm up.

Unfortunately, it's not easy to predict when a class will take place. Sometimes shows run slowly and it seems to take forever for your class to start. But if a show has few entries it will go faster. Better to get to the show with too much time to spare than too little!

To save time, put on your show gear at home. Wear a pair of baggy sweatpants over your jodhpurs and boots to keep them clean.

TRAILERING

If your horse must ride in a trailer to get to a show, he should wear traveling gear. Padded boots on his legs protect him from bumps and cuts. The boots should cover his knees and hocks and a little bit of his hooves. If your horse rubs his rear end in the trailer, wrap a stretchy tail bandage around his tail to keep it neat. This bandage starts at the top of the tail and stops at the end of the tailbone, halfway down.

If the show is a couple of hours away, hang a hay net in the trailer so your horse has something to nibble on.

Your pony should wear protective shipping gear in the trailer.

SHOW STAFF

When you go to a show, knowing who is in charge comes in handy. Let's take a look at some of the people who work at a show.

Manager: the organizer of the show. This is the person in charge!

Judge: the person who evaluates the riders and horses and awards ribbons.

Ring steward: the person who makes sure all the rules are followed at the show.

Announcer: the person with the microphone.

Course designer: the person who designs and helps to set up jumping courses.

Secretary: the person who sits in the show office and takes your entry form and money.

Volunteers: most shows have volunteers, people who help out but don't get paid. Make sure you're nice to everyone who is lending a hand. Most volunteers work at shows because they love horses or they are friends with competitors who ride. They may open and shut gates, work as the jump crew, or hand out ribbons.

Left: *The judge decides who wins the ribbons.*
Above: *Always be polite and friendly to volunteers.*

ARRIVING

When you arrive, leave your horse in the trailer, and go to the office to pay your entry fees and collect your number, a card you'll pin or tie with a string on the back of your jacket. If you ask nicely, maybe Mom or Dad will take care of business and you can look after your horse.

Unload your horse and let him have a quick look round. Tie him to a ring on the trailer with a safety string loop and a quick-release knot and take off his shipping gear.

GROOMING

Your horse should be clean when you arrive at the show so he shouldn't need much grooming. Here's what you must do:

1. Pick out his feet. Don't put on hoof oil until right before your class.

2. Check that his braids are neat and tidy, and give his tail a quick brushing.

3. If his tail isn't braided, dampen the top of it and smooth down flyaway hair with human hair gel.

4. Use a body brush.

5. Fill a bucket with water and use a sponge to clean his eyes and dock area.

6. For extra shine, spray show conditioner (usually not allowed at 4-H shows) on him and buff him up with a towel. Don't spray where the saddle goes because the area will get slippery.

7. If he has white stockings, rub some baby powder on them to brighten them up.

Opposite Top: *After unloading your pony, take off the shipping boots or bandages.*
Opposite Bottom: *Collect your number from the show secretary.*
Above Left: *Clean your pony's eyes with a sponge.*
Above Right: *In summer, spray some fly repellent on your pony.*

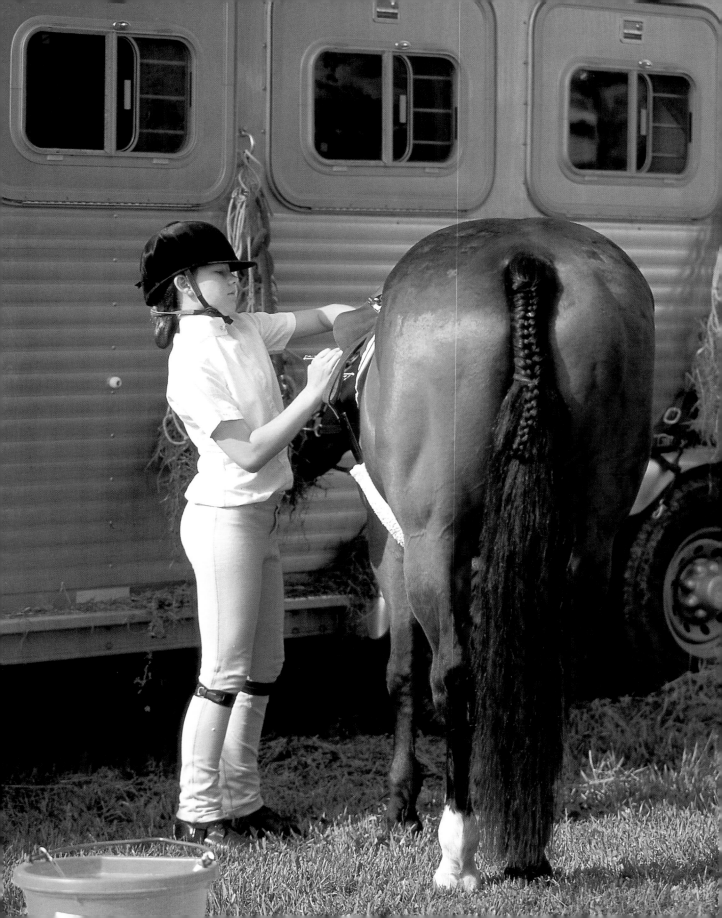

TACKING UP

Put the bridle on first, then the martingale, if your horse wears one. Put the halter over the bridle so you can keep your horse tied to the trailer while you put on his saddle. Take away his hay net so he doesn't chew on hay and get his bit dirty. Once he's tacked up, double check to make sure all bridle straps are secured in their keepers. Ask a pal to wipe any dust off your bridle and saddle with a clean rag.

HOP ON

Now's the time to take off your sweats, put on your showing jacket, and tie or pin your number to your back. Fasten your helmet and hop into the saddle. If you have time, walk your horse around the grounds for about ten minutes to help him get used to the hustle and bustle of the show. If he acts frisky, keep a firm rein on him, push him forward with your legs, and keep him away from other horses.

Stay alert on the show grounds. There will be people walking around, dogs barking (and they are not always on leashes as they are supposed to be), and people zipping by on motorbikes and golf carts. There are hazards everywhere! Unfortunately, people aren't always as considerate as they should be, but you should try your best to maintain good riding manners. Keep your eyes open and try to stay out of everyone's way.

Left: *Give yourself plenty of time to tack up.*
Above: *Ride your pony around the show ground so he gets used to the hustle and bustle.*

WARMING UP

Every show should have a warm-up arena, a ring close to the show ring where people school their horses before their classes. If the show has jumping classes, there will be a fence or two in the ring.

Be careful in the warm-up arena, especially if it's small. People forget to look where they are going and there are often collisions! Keep your distance from other competitors, and, just as in a lesson, always pass on the right. This means your left arm is closest to the other rider. If a person is coming up behind you, they may say "inside" or "outside" to let you know where they are going.

HEADS UP!

Listen for riders who say "heads up." This means they are going to jump a fence and don't want you in their way. If you want to jump a fence, say, "Heads up over the jump," and people should move. Some people just yell out the name of the fences they are jumping, for example, "Brush box to the vertical!" and everyone should get out of their way.

PREPARE YOURSELF

Walk around the warm-up ring a couple of times, then pick up a trot. Trot around the arena, then school your horse like you do at home. Do some circles and figure eights. Do some transitions such as walk to canter and trot to halt. Keep your horse working and paying attention to you. Canter on both leads.

The warm-up is a last-minute preparation for your class. It's a chance to make sure your horse is listening to you before you head off into the ring. It's also an opportunity for him to get rid of any excess energy.

If you're jumping, pop over the warm-up fences a couple of times. Check that the fence isn't too high. Don't jump a 3-foot warm-up fence if you're only jumping 2 feet 3 inches in your class. If the fence is too high, make sure no one else is jumping it and ask someone to lower it for you.

Trot over the fence once or twice, then pick up a canter. Give your horse plenty of room in front of the fence and approach it straight on. Once you land on the other side, urge your horse to go forward. Don't just let him stop. Give him a big pat if he's good. If he knocks the fence down, it's *your* responsibility to put it up again. Get off and do it or ask a pony pal to put it up.

Don't ride your horse to death in the warm-up ring. You shouldn't need more than a half hour to forty-five minutes. Your

Jump the warm-up fence only three or four times.

horse should have a little spring in his step when he gets in the ring. If he's naughty, take him on a five-minute walk around the show ground and come back and try again. Never lose your temper, and don't end your warm-up session on a bad note.

While you're warming up, keep one ear open to the loudspeaker. You don't want to miss the announcer calling your class to the ring.

TRAINER TIPS

If you bring your trainer to the show, he or she may come into the warm-up arena to help you. Your trainer will put up jumps and pick them up if you knock them down. He or she may help other students too. Your trainer will give you a few last-minute tips to think about before you compete. A good trainer is calm and supportive in the warm-up arena. He or she should give you extra confidence before your class. If your trainer yells at you or makes you nervous, then that person is not the trainer for you!

Your trainer should make you feel confident before a class.

CHAPTER SIX

SHOWING ON THE FLAT

Before you enter a show ring, you must have total control over your horse. At home, you must be able to walk, trot, and canter him without his bolting or bucking you off! A judge may ask you to leave the ring if your horse is naughty and upsetting the other horses.

Your horse should be well behaved around other horses. Although it is tolerated if he pins his ears back or acts grumpy in company, he shouldn't kick or lunge at others. Make sure you have ridden him several times with other horses before you venture out to a show.

LAST-MINUTE CHECKS

Before you enter the ring, ask a pony pal to give your boots a last-minute polish with a rag. Make sure all the straps on your bridle are in their keepers. Finally, make sure your number is on straight and fastened securely so it doesn't flop all over the place.

If you think your horse may kick if someone gets too close, tie a red ribbon around the top of his tail to warn other riders that they should steer clear of him.

Left: Ask a pal to give your boots a last-minute polish.

TIME TO ENTER THE RING

Get to the ring on time and walk in. Don't trot or canter because you may bump into other competitors who are trying to enter the ring too. Go in the same direction that everyone else is going. Try to position yourself near the fence and away from other horses. If you need to trot to get to a better space, go ahead, the judge won't mind. Think about your position. Even though the class hasn't started yet, the judge may be looking at you.

In most flat classes you'll have a few minutes to organize yourself before the judge begins the class. Place your hands close to your horse's neck and straighten your back. Pretend there's a string pulling your head upward. Push down your heels.

Once the ring steward announces that the class has begun, you must wait for the judge's commands. Usually the first command is to walk. Squeeze with your legs, so your horse moves in a nice, active manner. Don't let him slop along with his nose on the ground!

After you've walked around the ring once or twice, the steward will say, "trot." Ask your horse to trot in the same calm way you would at home. You don't want him to get excited and canter. You'll lose marks. Immediately check that you are on the correct diagonal. A judge will notice if you are on the wrong one. Look down with your eyes—not your whole head!—and make sure that you are rising when your horse's outside foreleg is forward. If you are on the wrong diagonal, quietly sit in the saddle for two beats and then begin rising to the trot again. In some classes you may be asked to do a sitting trot, so be prepared.

When the steward asks you to canter, make sure you have plenty of space and give the correct aids. Quickly check that you are on the correct lead. Your horse's inside foreleg should reach farther forward than his outside leg. If your horse is on the wrong lead, don't panic. Simply bring him back to a trot, and ask for the canter again. You hope that the judge didn't see the mistake! Don't circle and make a big deal out of the error.

Once you've walked, trotted, and cantered in one direction, the steward will ask you to reverse. Some people like to do a turn on the forehand to impress the judge, but if you don't know how to do one, just make a small loop to the inside and reverse your direction. Then you'll be asked to walk, trot, and canter again.

Make sure your pony is moving forward at an active pace.

LOOK AT ME!

If you and your horse are doing well, you want the judge to notice! Stay away from the other competitors so that when you pass the judge you're all by yourself. If you're getting too close to someone, pass the person on the inside or make a circle. Don't spend all of your time circling or cutting across the arena, because you won't be able to show off in front of the judge.

Be considerate of the other competitors. Don't cut anyone off or get too close. Look cheerful. Try to have fun while you are in the ring. You don't have to glue a phony smile on your face, but you don't have to look miserable either. After all, you're very lucky to have a horse to ride and the opportunity to be in a show. A lot of kids would like to be you!

Keep plenty of space between you and the competitor in front of you.

WORKING HUNTER ON THE FLAT OR UNDER SADDLE

In a working hunter under-saddle class, your horse is judged. The judge looks at your horse's manners and the way he moves. Your horse should be well balanced and look like he is comfortable to ride. If your horse bumps you ten feet out of the saddle when he trots, he may not be suitable for a working hunter class. You must have light contact on your horse's mouth. Your horse will be marked down if he looks grumpy and hard to ride. Even though the judge is not paying much attention to you in this class, you should still concentrate on looking polished and professional.

You may be asked to hand gallop in a working hunter class. Usually the steward asks everyone to line up before asking for this speedy gait. Then each person goes on the track individually and hand gallops for the judge. Watch what the other competitors are doing to figure out where you should hand gallop.

To ask your horse to hand gallop, first pick up the canter. Then sit slightly forward and encourage him forward with your legs. He should stick his nose out a bit and pick up speed.

EQUITATION ON THE FLAT

Your riding skill is judged in an equitation class. A judge looks at your position and the way you ride your horse. If your hands are flying all over the place and you're bouncing in the air, the judge will mark you down. Ride along quietly and don't bring too much attention to yourself. Use a shorter rein in an equitation class than you would in a hunter class.

You may be asked to ride without stirrups, sit the trot, and post to the extended trot in an equitation class.

The judge studies your riding skills in an equitation class.

THE LINE UP

When the class is almost over, the judge asks you to line up. Usually you line up in the middle of the ring, facing away from the judge so he or she can see your number clearly. Don't line up too close to another horse because your horse might fidget or argue with his neighbor.

The judge checks your number and makes his final decision. Then he hands the results to the steward who takes them to the announcer. The announcer calls out the results. If your number is called, walk to the steward or the person handing out the ribbons, take your ribbon and say, "Thank you!" Remember to give your horse a pat—he worked hard too. If you don't win a ribbon, be a good sport and smile on your way out. Nobody likes a sore loser!

Above: *Don't get too close to other horses in the line up.* Opposite Top: *If you've done well, you might win a blue ribbon!* Opposite Bottom: *Your trainer will want to discuss the class with you.*

AFTER THE CLASS

When you've left the ring, talk to your trainer. She or he may have noticed a mistake or two that you made without knowing. Your trainer may also want to congratulate you!

Don't run off and sulk if you didn't do well. And don't complain to the judge about your score. He or she will not change it. If the judge wants to talk to you about the class, he or she may do it while you're in the ring or after the class.

If your horse is going into another class shortly, ride him to the warm-up arena and school him if necessary. If you don't want to school him, ride him around the show ground at a walk to keep him busy. If you have a few minutes between classes, hop off and loosen his girth to give him a break.

If you're done for a while, ride your horse back to the trailer and untack him. Give him a drink of water and a nibble of hay.

RIBBON COLORS	
FIRST	blue
SECOND	red
THIRD	yellow
FOURTH	white
FIFTH	pink
SIXTH	green
SEVENTH	purple
EIGHTH	brown
NINTH	gray
TENTH	light blue

TALKING TO THE JUDGE

If your trainer or parents don't understand why you placed as you did and they feel that they must talk to the judge, they should go to the show organizer or manager and request to speak to the judge. Some judges are willing to talk to competitors and explain their reasons for the ribbon order in a class.

At big shows it will probably be quite difficult to chat with judges, but at little shows, they probably won't mind. If your parents are angry about your placing, it's best if they take a few minutes to cool down before talking to the judge. It's important that your parents behave in a sportsmanlike manner too. Nobody likes to be around a badly behaved show mom or dad!

At bigger shows, you may not be able to discuss your placing with the judge.

CHAPTER SEVEN

JUMPING

If you plan to jump at a show, you must be able to jump your horse at your own barn. You should enjoy jumping him and feel 100 percent safe popping over fences. When you look at the schedule, pick classes with fence heights that you are used to jumping. If you jump 2 feet 6 inches at home, don't try to jump 3 feet at a show. "Over jumping" your horse can ruin all the good work you've done at home.

There are many classes with different fence heights to choose from, and there should be one that is perfect for you and your horse. You could do a cross-rail class, in which the fences are tiny cross-rails decorated with flowers or brush. Cross-rail jumps are usually no higher than 1 1/2 foot—perfect for first-time show jumpers. If you like to jump higher, there are pony jumper classes in which you can jump up to 3 feet 6 inches.

Left: *Don't jump show fences that are higher than the ones you jump at home.*
Above: *A pony can get speedy when jumping, and you may have to use a strong bit like a Kimberwicke on him.*

MEMORIZING THE COURSE

Show organizers post show-jumping courses outside the ring. Give yourself a few minutes to memorize the course. Ask someone to hold your horse while you give the course diagram a good look. In most jumping classes, you can walk the course without your horse before you ride. If your trainer is helping you, he or she should walk the course with you.

When you enter the ring on foot, decide how you are going to approach the first fence. Figure out which lead you will need to be on, and decide where you are going to pick it up. Look at each fence. Are there any that might scare your horse? If a fence looks spooky, you may need extra leg when you approach it. Count strides in between fences so you know how many strides your horse should take to jump nicely.

Left: *Walking the course lets you look at each fence close up.*
Right: *Take a few minutes to memorize your course.*

COUNTING STRIDES

Here is a rough guide to help you learn how to count strides. A stride is the length or distance your horse travels with each step at any of the gaits. At home, grab a measuring tape and choose which stride fits your horse or pony:

A big horse's stride is about 12 to 13 feet.
Small horse or large pony: 11 feet.
Small or medium pony: 9 to 10 feet.

Unwind the tape and mark off the length of your horse's stride. Practice walking the length of the stride. Most people take big steps when walking a stride. Count how many of your steps it takes to walk one of your horse's strides and try to remember this number when you are walking a course. At the first fence, you'll want to start the jump about a stride away because your horse lands a couple of feet from the fence. Also, finish a stride away from the second fence.

A few minutes before the class begins, the steward will post a list of competitors and the order in which they will jump. If you are first, don't panic! Go in and do the best job you can. If you are farther down the list, watch a few people ride the course. Spot where competitors are having problems and try to avoid those glitches when you ride the course.

THE COURTESY CIRCLE

When you enter the ring, it's a good idea to do a courtesy circle (sometimes called a hunter circle). This is when you trot in a big circle and pick up your canter, if you are cantering, before you head for the first fence. Doing a courtesy circle gives you a chance to get your horse on the correct lead and establish the pace for your round. If your horse is lazy, tap him with the whip behind your leg to wake him up. If your horse is zippy, sit deep in the saddle and try to slow him down.

After you jump the last fence, do another circle. This lets you slow down gradually and gracefully. Watch other competitors to see where they make their circles.

Left: *How many steps make up one of your pony's strides?*
Right: *Do a courtesy circle before you head for the first fence.*

HUNTER CLASSES

Hunter courses are usually easy to memorize. There are generally eight or nine fences. You'll probably go up a long side with two fences, down a diagonal, up a side, and down another diagonal.

In hunter classes, your horse is judged on his performance, manners, style of jumping, and way of going.

If two horses go clear over a hunter course, the one that did it with the best style will place higher. Rubbing or knocking a pole will lose you marks, even if it does not fall down

A GOOD HUNTER HORSE:	A BAD HUNTER HORSE:
• canters around the course at an even pace;	• gallops around the course at top speed;
• is well behaved;	• throws his head around;
• tucks legs up over fences;	• refuses a fence;
• looks interested in what he's doing.	• looks grumpy and uncomfortable.

The fences in hunter classes are usually made of natural materials such brush or green plants.

EQUITATION CLASSES

The rider is the one being judged in an equitation class. Your position must be picture perfect. The judge will be looking at how you ride the minute you enter the ring and start to do your courtesy circle. The judge will note if you look in control of your horse and if you are setting him up to take the jumps nicely. If he jumps sloppily or he refuses a jump—even if you look great—you'll be penalized.

The course in an equitation class may be more complicated than in a hunter class.

A GOOD EQUITATION RIDER:	A BAD EQUITATION RIDER:
• keeps her hands near the horse's neck;	• flaps her arms;
• looks straight ahead over fences;	• looks down over a fence;
• keeps her legs still;	• has wiggly legs;
• sits quietly in the saddle.	• bumps around like a sack of potatoes!

The judge checks out your position over each fence in an equitation class.

JUMPER CLASSES

The only thing that counts in a jumper class is going around clear—no refusals or knockdowns—in the time allowed. The styles of the horse and rider aren't judged. This is why you may see some rough riding in jumper classes. Some riders care more about getting over each fence than they do about their position. They may yell to encourage their horse over a tough fence.

Jumper courses are trickier than courses in hunter or equitation classes. There might be a triple fence (three fences close together) or some sharp turns in the course. You may have to jump the same fence twice from different directions.

Jumper classes usually consist of two rounds. If more than one rider goes clear in the first round, then it is required that the riders jump a shorter course while being timed. A jump-off usually has five or six fences. They'll be the same fences that were jumped in the first round but this time they may be in a different order. The horse that goes around the jump-off with the fastest time and the fewest penalties wins the blue ribbon. If you go clear but take too long or take longer than the time allowed, you'll be penalized.

If you make it to the jump-off, study the shortened course. Don't get confused and pop over a fence that isn't in the jump-off. You'll be disqualified. Some shows make you stay in the ring after you have a clear round and then have you jump the jump-off course immediately. This is so classes move quickly. You may want to

memorize both the jumper course and the jump-off course before you enter the arena. Don't panic if you have to do the jump-off right away. Your horse is warmed up and should jump nicely, but remember that speed is important.

Even though you may see other people going wild in jumper classes, stay calm and maintain a good position. You'll upset

your horse if you're flapping around like a maniac. He may knock down a fence. You should know your horse well enough to know if he needs a kick or a tap with the crop. Ride him as you do at home.

You may pick up a lot of speed during a jumper class so you must be able to slow your horse down. When you've cleared the last fence, don't haul on your horse's mouth to stop him. Bring him back to a canter, and then trot him around before you leave the ring. When you exit the ring, walk your horse until he calms down and cools off.

You are timed in a jump-off.

REFUSALS AND ELIMINATION

If your horse stops in front of a jump or runs away from it, this is called a refusal. Don't panic or get upset. Simply circle your horse away from the jump, then try again. Make a small circle, and don't give your horse a lot of time or space to think about refusing again.

If your horse refuses more than three times, you're eliminated. The announcer will say, "Thank you," and you must walk out of the ring. Don't get mad and whip your horse. Say thanks to the judge or nod at him or her and leave. Some judges may let you jump an easier fence before you leave the arena, so you finish up on a good note. As you walk out, think about what you need to work on when you get home.

If you go off course (take the fences in the wrong order), you'll be eliminated, but if you fall off, dust yourself off and remount. Don't cry or make a fuss. If you're competing at a USA Equestrian show or one that follows USA Equestrian rules, you'll be eliminated, and you must leave the ring. If you're competing at a smaller show, look at the judge and ask her if you can continue. She may let you finish the course, or she may tell you that you can jump a "courtesy fence." This means you can jump one fence and then you must leave the ring. Jumping a courtesy fence lets you and your horse finish on a positive note.

Don't freak out if you have a refusal or a runout.

CHAPTER EIGHT

AFTER THE CLASS

If you have another class in a few minutes, stay in the saddle and walk around to keep your horse supple and ready to go. If your next class isn't for a while, dismount, loosen your horse's girth, and stand in the shade if it's sunny. If you have enough time, take him back to the trailer, tie him up, and untack him. Give him a quick grooming and offer him some water. If he's missed his lunch give him a small feed or a full hay net.

Once your horse is settled, don't just run off and leave him. Make sure there is a person stationed at the trailer in case something goes wrong. And store your tack and clothing out of sight in the trailer. Shows are easy places for thieves to nab riding gear.

Bring a comfy fold-up chair and a newspaper for your parent. He or she can guard the trailer while you wander around the show ground.

TIME TO LEAVE

When you've finished at the show, pack your gear and put on your horse's shipping boots. Check that he has hay to munch in the trailer. If your horse has pooped all over the place, find a pitchfork and put the droppings on the show ground muck heap. Leave your trailer parking spot clean and tidy.

When you arrive at home, unload your horse and give him another quick grooming. Check him from head to hoof to make sure he did not scratch or injure himself in the trailer.

Try to stick to your horse's normal schedule. If it's near his feeding time, give him his feed. If not, put him in his field so he can have a well-deserved roll or gallop to let off some steam. Watch him for a few minutes to make sure he is A-OK after his day at the show, and give him the next day off so he has a chance to unwind.

Opposite: Muck out your trailer before the trip home.
Above Left: Give your pony a hay net to nibble on when he's tied to the trailer.
Above Right: Always keep an eye on the trailer and your gear.

HOW DID YOU DO?

Now you can analyze your showing performance. Don't worry if you didn't win a ribbon. Remember, winning isn't everything. If you were pleased with the way your horse behaved at the show, you should be happy. You'll win a ribbon eventually!

You should be thrilled if your horse was calm and well behaved, friendly to other horses, steady in the ring, and happy to jump all the fences put in front of him. Your show experience was a success if he halted when you asked him to and stood quietly when tied to the trailer.

If your horse wasn't perfectly behaved, don't run out and put an ad in the newspaper to sell him. Try to figure out why he was naughty at the show. You may have been part of the problem. Perhaps you were nervous and upset him. Maybe you didn't ride as well as you do at home. Perhaps you asked him to do things he wasn't ready to do or tried things you hadn't practiced at home.

If he was just being stubborn and obnoxious, don't give up on him. He may need to go to more shows to gain experience. Maybe you need to be firmer with him. If you don't let him get away with bad behavior at home, then he'll be less likely to try it at a show. If he was really bad, arrange to take him to another show but don't enter him in any classes. Lunge him for about half an hour, then ride him around the show grounds. Take him in the warm-up arena if he's behaving himself. If it's a local show, ask your trainer to come and give you a lesson on the show ground.

If your horse is a bit naughty at shows, stick to smaller events until his behavior improves. Organizers tend to be very strict at large shows, and they won't like your horse fooling around. People may be more helpful and understanding at a small show.

Above Left: You should be pleased if your pony was quiet and well behaved at the show.
Above Right: Take your green horse to smaller shows so he can get used to the noise and activity.
Opposite: If you had problems with a fence at a show, make one like it at home.

YOUR NEXT LESSON

Talk about the show with your trainer at your next lesson. He or she may not have had a lot of time at the show to chat with you. Your trainer should be able to tell you what you did well and what things you need to practice. Your trainer should have a positive attitude about the show and should encourage you to have one too!

If you had a problem with a particular fence at a show, ask your trainer to build a similar fence at home and practice popping your horse over it. Buy plastic flowers and decorate the fence. Cut some branches from a fir tree and put them in front of a jump. You may have to practice counting strides in between fences if you forgot to do it at the show. Your trainer can also ask you to do some of the things the judge asked you to do during a class, like a sitting trot or riding on a loose rein.

You and your trainer can also discuss when you will go to a show again and what classes you may want to enter. That'll give you a fun goal to work toward.

Left: *Your horse may need extra schooling before you go to another show.*
Right: *Work with your trainer to get ready for the next show.*

CHAPTER NINE

ORGANIZING A FUN SHOW

If you love showing, and you keep your horse at a boarding barn where there are other kids, you could organize your own small show. Talk to a few of your pony pals and your trainer, and see if they would be willing to assist. If they agree to help, talk to the barn owner or manager and ask if they would allow you to hold a fun show. Tell them that the show would be only for people who board at the barn. They'll have to make sure the barn's insurance will cover the show. They may have to look into hiring a medical emergency team for the day. If they like the idea of a small show, get together with your friends and think up some classes that would be fun.

FUN CLASSES

Here are some examples of classes you could hold:

Costume class: Riders dress up themselves and their ponies in funny costumes. The most inventive pony and rider win first prize.

Showmanship: Competitors are judged on how neat and professional they look in

their show clothes and how well groomed and turned-out their ponies are.

Equitation on the flat: Everyone is judged at the walk, trot, and canter.

Equitation over fences: Set up a small course and everyone can pop over it. The person who has the best round wins.

Left: You can really get creative with your costume!
Right: Costume classes are tons of fun.

Lead line: Dress up your little brother or sister and lead them around on your pony.

Ride a buck: Everyone rides bareback with a dollar stuck in between her pony and her thigh. Everyone must walk, trot, and canter when asked to by the judge. The person who keeps the buck under her leg the longest wins all the money!

Handy pony: Set up a short obstacle course, and the pony that goes through it most calmly wins. Here are some things that can be included in the obstacle course:

• putting a letter in a mailbox
• taking clothing off a line
• walking over a plastic trash bag on the

Above Top: *Both you and your pony need to sparkle in a showmanship class.*
Bottom: *Don't worry if you don't have a show jacket at a fun show. A polo top is fine.*

ground (make sure someone secures the bag with two poles)
- carrying a cup of water over three or four poles on the ground
- opening and shutting a gate without dismounting
- jumping a tiny jump
- putting on a raincoat

Musical buckets: Just like musical chairs, except you have to get your pony to the bucket, hop off, and put one foot on the bucket. One bucket is taken away each round. You'll need a cassette player or a radio for this class.

Above Top: *A handy pony should help you open and close a gate.*
Bottom: *Musical buckets is one fun game you can play.*

HERE COMES THE JUDGE!

You'll need a judge at your show. You could ask your trainer if he or she knows of any outside trainers who would come to your barn and judge for a small fee. If the show is going to last a few hours, you'll have to provide lunch for the judge. Make the judge a sandwich and give him or her a bag of potato chips, and a soft drink or water. The judge won't be able to concentrate on judging if he or she is hungry! Maybe you could ask someone's parents to donate a yummy lunch for the judge.

SHOW PROGRAM

Now you have to decide when you'd like to have your show. Weekends are usually best for shows because working moms and dads can help. But if you are holding the show during riding camp, you can have the show on a weekday.

When you've decided on a date and what classes you're going to have, make a show program on a computer. Include the following on your program:
- date of the show and starting time
- judge of the show
- classes being held at the show
- cost of the classes
- the name and phone number of the person in charge of the show so people can ask questions

You'll need to decide how much the entry fees are going to be at your show. Keep them low. Remember, this is a fun show. A dollar or two should be fine. Once the program is finished, print out a few copies and post it on the bulletin board at your barn.

RIBBONS AND PRIZES

Before your show, ask everybody to donate some of their old ribbons. You can use these for the winners. Don't worry about what color they are. If you get a lot of ribbons, you can decide how many placings there will be in each class. If you get a ton of ribbons, you might be able to have first through fifth place. If you don't get many ribbons, you might only be able to award first place. If you want to give prizes to the class winners, you could give them small horsey items.

If you're feeling very motivated, you could go to the local tack shop or feed store and ask if the owner would like to sponsor a class and provide a prize. Tell the owner that she can come to the show and present the prize to the class winner.

SAMPLE HORSEY PRIZES

- **brushes**
- **bag of apples**
- **bag of carrots**
- **hoof oil**
- **horse shampoo**

Left: *You'll need a judge at your show.*
Above: *Post your show program at the barn where people can see it.*

VOLUNTEERS

Round up moms, dads, brothers, sisters, and grandparents to help at your show. You'll need people to open gates, set up jumps, organize the handy pony course, collect the entry fees, and hand out ribbons—little brothers and sisters are very good at handing out prizes! Remember to be very nice and say, "Thank you," to anyone who volunteers at your show.

PROFITS

If your show makes a profit, you can do several things with the money. Put it in the bank and use it to finance your next show. Or better yet, you could donate the profits to a horse charity or your local humane society. Since horses and other furry creatures are such a big part of your life, it would be nice to give something back to them.

You could also donate some money to your local Riding for the Handicapped program so that mentally and physically challenged people can enjoy horses and riding as much as you do.

Younger siblings come in handy for giving out ribbons.

CHAPTER TEN

SHOWING PROBLEMS & HOW TO AVOID OR SOLVE THEM

Going to a show can be a big effort. It involves a lot of organization, and the entry fees can sometimes cost a lot of money. That's why it can be very frustrating when something goes wrong. In this final chapter, let's look at some showing problems and ways that you can solve them.

You get your pony out of the trailer and he's got a big manure stain on his leg:

Always take equine spot or stain remover to a show. Spray some on the spot, work it in with a sponge, and wipe it off with a clean cloth.

You can't find your gloves and crop: Make a list of things you need to bring to the show, and while you are packing the trailer, check off the items as you load them. Tape a copy of the list inside your trailer door, and use it every time you go to a show.

Opposite: *Keep plenty of room between you and the other riders in a flat class.*
Above Left: *Got a gray or pinto pony? Don't leave home without green stain remover!*
Above Right: *Make a list and check it twice so you don't leave any show gear at home.*

Your girth strap breaks before a class:
Always bring an extra girth and set of reins
in case either breaks at a show. Always
bring an extra halter and lead rope too, in
case your horse pulls back from the trailer,
breaks his halter, and runs off.

**In a flat class you keep getting stuck
behind a slowpoke:** Pass the slowpoke to
the inside and try to stay in front of them.
Give the other people plenty of room.

**You have a refusal while competing in a
jumping class:** Turn your horse around, give
him a sharp tap with the crop behind your
leg, and head for the fence again. Don't give
your horse a big approach to the fence or

time to think about refusing again. Don't
ever beat or lose your temper with your
horse—inside or outside the show arena.

You fall off during a class: If you're not
hurt, catch your pony as quickly as you
can and remount. If you're at a rated show,
or one following USA Equestrian rules,
you'll be eliminated and asked to leave the
arena. If you're at a smaller show, look at
the judge and ask if you may continue
competing in the class. At small, unrated
shows, a judge may let you finish the class
or course. Try to act as if you haven't fall-
en off. Don't make a big scene and bawl
your eyes out!

Above: *If you have a refusal, approach the fence again immediately.*
Right: *If you think you've knocked down a pole, don't look back to check it.*

If another competitor falls off, you and the other riders should stand still and wait for the rider or a ring steward to catch the horse.

Your horse runs out of the ring: If the class has begun, you may be eliminated. Look at the judge and see if he or she will let you re-enter the ring and finish your class. If you notice that the gate is open after you've entered the arena, ask someone to shut it before you begin your round.

You almost crash into someone while jumping the warm-up fence: Warn people that you are going to be jumping a fence. For instance, yell, "Brush box to brick wall, please!" and everyone should get out of your way.

You jump over the warm-up fence in the wrong direction: This can get you eliminated at some events. Always jump with the red flag on your right. Make sure you look at the fence carefully before jumping it.

You think you've knocked a pole over while jumping a course: Forget about the pole and don't look back. Focus on the course ahead, and give your horse an extra kick to get him going forward.

You forget to bring a copy of your horse's Coggin's test: You'll probably have to go home and get it. Some shows won't let you compete unless you've got a copy of the Coggin's test, a test a veterinarian does to make sure your horse doesn't have equine infectious anemia. Make several copies of the Coggin's test. Keep one in your truck, one in your trailer, and one in your parent's car—just in case!

You're competing in a division and you arrive late for the first class: Don't panic. You can still compete in the other classes of the division. You just won't be able to win a championship ribbon. In the future, give yourself more time to get to a show. You could get caught in traffic, your horse might not load, or you could forget an important piece of tack. Always try to arrive at least an hour before your first class.

Your horse kicks another horse at a show: Apologize profusely and do your best to keep your pony away from other horses. If others get too close to you, tell them that your horse may kick and that they should keep their distance. If it is a casual show, you can tie a red ribbon on your horse's tail to warn others to stay clear.

A red ribbon warns other riders to stay back from a potential kicker.

You forget your show-jumping course: Slow down a bit and remain calm. Look back at the last fence you jumped and try to remember where the next fence is. If you go off-course, you will be eliminated, but first nod your head at the judge to salute, then leave the arena. The next time you jump, walk the course several times if you can, and then study the course, or watch a few rounds, until you know it by heart.

You feel extremely nervous and can't concentrate: Go to a quiet area in the warm-up arena and walk in a circle with your horse. Try to calm down. Breathe in and out slowly. Think about your next class and plan how you are going to ride. Remember that showing is supposed to be fun, and winning isn't everything.

If you're jumping, watch two or three competitors ride around the course to help you memorize it. There's no need to be nervous if you know your course.

Left: *Feeling nervous? Go to a quiet area and take a break with your horse.*
Right: *Study the course diagram and watch a round or two before you enter the ring.*

FINAL ROUND

Now that you've read this book, you should feel pretty confident about going to your first show. You've done your homework and know exactly what to expect once you arrive on the show grounds. You've spent a lot of time in the saddle, and you and your favorite horse are a perfect team. You've rustled up some showing clothes, and the tack that you're going to use is neat and tidy. You're prepared.

Here are a few showing rules that will help you have fun on the big day:

- Be a good sport. Even though it's cool to win a ribbon, you might not always take one home. Don't be a grump if you don't win something.
- Remember to put your horse's comfort before your own. Offer him a drink of water before you run for a soda.
- Be nice to your family and friends who help you.
- Smile a lot, and have a great time!

So, what are you waiting for? Head on down to the local tack shop to pick up some show programs, and find an event that has classes that suit you and your four-legged friend. You're ready to go to a show!

Being well prepared is the key to winning ribbons.

**American Association for
Horsemanship Safety**
P.O. Box 39
Fentress, TX 78622
(512) 488-2220
www.law.utexas.edu/dawson

**American Connemara
Pony Society**
2630 Hunting Ridge Road
Winchester, VA 22603
(540) 662-5953
www.acps.org

**American Grandprix
Association**
3104 Cherry Palm Drive,
Suite 220
Tampa, FL 33619
(813) 623-5801

American Horse Council
1700 L Street NW, Suite 300
Washington,
DC 20006-3805
(202) 296-4031
www.horsecouncil.org

**American Miniature
Horse Association**
5601 South Interstate 35W
Alvarado, TX 76009
(817) 783-5600
www.amha.org

**American Morgan
Horse Association**
P.O. Box 960
Shelburne VT 05482
(802) 985-4944
www.morganhorse.com

**American Paint
Horse Association**
P.O. Box 961023
Fort Worth, TX 76161
(817) 439-3400
www.apha.com

**American Quarter
Horse Association**
P.O. Box 200
Amarillo, TX 79168
(800) 414-RIDE
www.aqha.com

**American Riding Instructors
Association**
28801 Trenton Court
Bonita Springs, FL 34134
(941) 948-3232
www.riding-instructor.com

**American Youth
Horse Council**
4193 Iron Works Pike
Lexington, KY 40511
(800) TRY-AYHC

**Appaloosa Horse
Club, Inc.**
P.O. Box 8403
Moscow, ID 83843
(208) 882-5578
www.appaloosa.com

**Arabian Horse
America**
12000 Zuni Street
Westminster, CO 80234
(877) 551-2722
www.arabianhorseamerica.com

Canadian Pony Club
Box 127
Baldur, Manitoba ROK
OBO
(888) 286-PONY
www.canadianponyclub.org

CHA—The Association for Horsemanship Safety and Education
5318 Old Bullard Road
Tyler, TX 75703
(800) 399-0138
www.cha-ahse.org

Future Farmers of America
P.O. Box 6890
Indianapolis, IN 46268-0960
(317) 802-6060
www.ffa.org

Intercollegiate Horse Show Association
P.O. Box 741
Stony Brook, NY 11790
(516) 751-2803
www.ihsa.com

The Jockey Club
821 Corporate Drive
Lexington, KY 40503
(800) 444-8521
www.jockeyclub.com

National 4-H Council
7100 Connecticut Avenue
Chevy Chase, MD 20815
(301) 961-2830
www.4h-usa.org

National Hunter and Jumper Association
P.O. Box 1015
Riverside, CT 06878
(203) 869-1225
www.nhja.com

North American Riding for the Handicapped Association
P.O. Box 33150
Denver, CO 80233
(800) 369-RIDE
www.narha.org

Pony of the Americas Club
5240 Elmwood Avenue
Indianapolis, IN 46203-5990
(317) 788-0107
www.poac.org

United States Equestrian Team
Gladstone, NJ 07934
(908) 234-1251
www.uset.com

The United States Pony Club
4071 Iron Works Pike
Lexington, KY 40511
(859) 254-PONY
www.ponyclub.org

Welsh Pony and Cob Society of America
P.O. Box 2977
Winchester, VA 22604-2977
(540) 667-6195
www.welshpony.org

USA Equestrian
4047 Iron Works Parkway
Lexington, KY 40511
(859) 258-2472
www.equestrian.org

Young Rider Magazine
P.O. Box 8237
Lexington, KY 40533
(859) 260-9800
www.youngrider.com

bit: the metal mouthpiece on a bridle

breastplate: a device of leather or nylon used across a horse's chest, attaches to the saddle and girth to prevent the saddle from slipping back

bridle: a head harness used to control and guide a horse when riding or driving

canter: a three-beat gait resembling a slow gallop

crop: a short riding whip with a looped lash

Coggin's test: a test given to detect equine anemia

course: a group of fences that are jumped in a particular order

courtesy circle: a circle done at the beginning and end of a jumping class

cross rails: a fence made of two poles that are crossed to make a low spot in the center of the fence

diagonal: when the horse's outside leg is moving forward at the trot, the rider should rise out of the saddle. If the rider is on the correct diagonal his horse will be more balanced

division: several classes that are linked together

elimination: when you are disqualified from a class and must leave the ring

equitation class: a class in which the rider, not the horse, is judged

flash noseband: a noseband with an extra piece of leather that fastens around a horse's

mouth so he can't open it and evade the bit

flat class: a class without fences to jump

faults: penalty points given to a competitor during a jumping round for knockdowns, refusals, poor jumping style, and exceeding the time allowed for the round

gag bit: an extra-strong bit that makes a horse raise his head

gag bridle: a corrective bridle; cheek pieces of rounded leather or rope pass through holes at the top and bottom of round bit rings before attaching to the reins

gait: the sequence in which a horse moves his feet in forward motion, including walk, trot, canter, and gallop

garters: leather straps that go around a rider's leg to prevent her jodhpurs from riding up

girth: a band that encircles a horse's belly to hold a saddle

green: an inexperienced horse

hand: a 4-inch measurement used to measure horses from the ground to the withers

halter: a head harness without a bit made out of leather or nylon

heads up: what competitors say when they want others to move out of their way

hand gallop: faster than a canter, but slower than a gallop

hunter class: a class in which the horse, not the rider, is judged

in-hand class: a class in which the competitor remains unmounted and leads the horse into the ring with a bridle or halter

inside leg: the one closest to the middle of the ring

jodhpurs: a style of stretchy riding pants that are close-fitting from knee to ankle

jumper class: a jumping class that is judged on speed and faults, including refusals or knockdowns

Kimberwicke bit: a bit that has a low port or snaffle, short cheek pieces, and curb chain

lead (as in the correct lead): when a horse canters, his inside foreleg should reach farther forward than his outside foreleg. A horse is more balanced if he is on the correct lead

line up: at the end of the class the competitors line up in the middle of the ring with their backs and numbers to the judge

lunge: when a person stands on the ground and works or exercises a horse in a circle around him or her by using a long line attached to the horse's head harness. Also spelled "longe."

martingale: a leather strap that attaches to the bridle's reins or a noseband, helping keep a horse from throwing his head in the air to avoid the bit

noseband: a strap of leather that goes around a horse's nose

outside leg: the one closest to the fence or wall around the ring

Pelham: a bit that has rings at the top and bottom ends of the cheek piece and is used with a snaffle and a curb, usually with two sets of reins

prize list: the list of classes and divisions that a horse show offers

ratcatcher: a special showing shirt with a detachable collar

refusal: when a horse refuses to jump an obstacle

schooling: warming up or training a horse

schooling show: an informal show, perfect for inexperienced riders or horses

snaffle bit: type of bit that may be either straight or broken

tack: saddle, bridle, and other equipment used in riding and handling a horse

trot: a natural two-beat gait in which the forefoot and diagonally opposite hind foot strike the ground simultaneously

under saddle: a class in which horses are ridden on the flat

turn on the forehand: a movement in which a horse's hind legs move around in a half circle while the forelegs stay in basically the same spot, sometimes used for reversing direction

walk: to move by alternately stepping in an even four-beat sequence

warm-up fence: a practice fence in the warm-up area outside the showing arena

Young Rider is the magazine that makes learning
about horses lots of fun!

Young Rider is packed with riding tips, horse-care hints, showing secrets,
breed profiles, and interviews with celebrity horses and riders.

Young Rider also contains competitions, freebies, pen pals
and special pages that spotlight our wonderful readers.
And each fun-filled issue has several gigantic color posters
of top riders and horses, cute foals, or amazing breeds!
To subscribe call 1 (800) 888-4421 or log onto
www.youngrider.com

Check out Lesley Ward's other horsey books from BowTie™ Press:
The Horse Illustrated Guide to Buying a Horse
The Horse Illustrated Guide to Caring for Your Horse
The Horse Illustrated Guide to Western Riding
The Horse Illustrated Guide to English Riding